Bobby Brewster and
the Magic Handyman

Bobby Brewster and the Magic Handyman

H. E. TODD

Illustrated by David Barnett

HODDER AND STOUGHTON
LONDON SYDNEY AUCKLAND TORONTO

British Library Cataloguing in Publication Data

Todd, H.E
    Bobby Brewster and the magic handyman.—(Brock red)
    I. Title   II. Barnett, David, *1931–*
    823'.914[J]   PZ7

    ISBN 0-340-39507-9

Text copyright © H. E. Todd 1987
Illustrations copyright © Hodder and Stoughton Ltd 1987

First published 1987

Published by Hodder and Stoughton Children's Books,
a division of Hodder and Stoughton Ltd,
Mill Road, Dunton Green, Sevenoaks, Kent TN13 2YJ

Photoset by Rowland Phototypesetting Ltd,
Bury St Edmunds, Suffolk

Printed in Great Britain by T. J. Press (Padstow) Ltd,
Padstow, Cornwall

Contents

My sincere thanks are due to Paul Ogden, who many years ago, after one of my school visits, sent me a story about a fantastic plumber. And also to Mr H. C. Mount, who at the same time sent a letter to the local paper about an equally fantastic little man on a tricycle who he picked out in the headlights of his car – and who then disappeared!

They stimulated me to write this book.

CHAPTER ONE

Bathroom taps

One morning, when Bobby Brewster's mother saw him at the breakfast table, she said, 'Bobby, you don't look very rested this morning.'

'I'm not,' he snapped. 'A wretched dripping tap in the bathroom kept me awake half the night. I hardly slept a wink.'

'Oh dear,' said his mother, 'I noticed that as well. I shall have to phone for a plumber.'

When she did, the manager of the shop explained that the usual plumber was on holiday. He had taken on a temporary man who would come during the morning.

Mrs Brewster wanted to pop next door to consult her neighbour about something.

She asked Bobby to stay indoors in case the plumber called so that he could explain what needed to be done. He was sitting reading a book when he heard the tinkling of a bell, and when he looked outside he saw an extraordinary sight.

Turning into the drive was a funny little man on a child's purple tricycle. He was dressed in the most colourful clothes, with a green coat, short blue trousers, yellow socks, and pink shoes with silver buckles. On his head was a knitted red hat with a multi-coloured bobble on top, and slung over one shoulder was a small crimson zip-bag. A little black and white dog with the cheekiest expression on his face was trotting beside him. The little man ran to the door with his dog still at his heels.

'Good morning, young man, I'm the plumber,' he said, sweeping his bobble-hat to the ground and bowing deeply, while the little dog woofed three times: 'Woof – woof – woof,' and wagged his tail.

'Excuse my saying so, but you don't

look like a plumber,' said Bobby. 'Where are your tools?'

'Here in my zip-bag,' replied the little man. Then he unzipped it and took out a red and white striped wand.

'Is that all?' asked Bobby in a surprised voice. 'You don't even know what the job is yet.'

'I can assure you, young man, that whatever the difficulty is my wand is quite adequate to cope with it,' the little man assured him. 'Please lead me to it, and my dog Impy must come too.'

They trooped up the staircase to the bathroom, where Bobby indicated the dripping tap.

'Ah, yes,' said the little man. 'We can soon put that right, can't we, Impy?' Then he tapped all four taps – two in the hand-basin and two in the bath – three times each with his striped wand, and announced clearly:

> 'Flop-flip,
> Make magic your drip.'

The little dog cocked his head on one side and woofed three times: 'Woof – woof – woof.' And immediately the tap stopped dripping!

'There, that will be satisfactory now,' said the little man, and they trooped back down the stairs, with Bobby too surprised to speak.

As they reached the hall his mother was

entering the house. Her mouth fell open with amazement when she saw the little man and his dog.

'Good morning, Mrs Brewster,' he said, again sweeping his bobble-hat to the ground and bowing deeply, while the little dog woofed three times.

Mrs Brewster stood tongue-tied.

'My dog Impy and I have just dealt satisfactorily with your dripping tap, madam,' he added. 'And I hope and believe that you will find everything to your complete satisfaction.'

Then he ran outside, vaulted on to his tricycle, and rode out of the drive, tinkling his bell, with the little dog beside him eagerly wagging his tail.

When Bobby's mother recovered her voice she exclaimed, 'Well, what an extraordinary sight! Such a funny little man and his perky little dog! But I've never seen a plumber like that before. Did he mend the tap?'

'Yes,' replied Bobby. 'He knocked it

three times with a red and white striped wand and said 'Flop-flip, make magic your drip.'

'He did *what*?' cried Mrs Brewster.

'He tapped it three times with a red and white striped wand and said 'Flop-flip, make magic your drip,' repeated Bobby. 'And then the tap stopped dripping.'

'I think I had better go and investigate,' said his mother. 'The whole thing seems extremely odd to me.'

They walked upstairs together and she was relieved to find that the offending tap was no longer dripping. But then a very funny thing happened. When she turned the tap on, out spurted an orange-coloured liquid. She put her finger in the stream and found that it was sticky – and when she licked her finger she tasted orange! There was no doubt about it – orangeade was pouring from the cold tap in the basin!

Then she tried the hot tap, and what do you think poured from that? Hot chocolate!

In the meantime Bobby had tried the taps in the bath. Out of the cold tap poured what looked like blackcurrant liquid, and from the hot tap streamed what un-doubtedly was sticky hot sweet lemon!

'It's all due to that odd little plumber and his dog,' cried Mrs Brewster. And Bobby had to agree.

At first they were quite excited. They

filled pots and pans and jugs with delicious liquids and arranged for neighbours to queue up for free drinks. But then they began to have doubts. Everything became sticky, and they wanted to wash their hands and couldn't. Bobby even started worrying about his next bath. Would he ever again be able to soak in luxury in lovely warm water?

Mrs Brewster became desperate and telephoned the shop again, but the manager said that the plumber who he had sent to the Brewster's earlier that day had never reported back to the shop. He simply couldn't understand it. It was very odd. Mrs Brewster replied crossly that it wasn't nearly as odd as her bathroom and rang off in a huff.

What on earth were they to do? They were stuck! And so would anyone be who tried to take a bath in sticky hot lemon!

The solution came later that morning. Bobby was out in the garden when he saw a little black and white dog. Hopefully he called 'Impy,' and the dog trotted up to him, wagging his tail. Then, when Impy barked happily, Mrs Brewster looked out of the kitchen window. She ran out and caught the little dog by his collar, and read the address on his name tag:

IMPY
FLOWER COTTAGE
LEAFY LANE

'You must take him home and ask that plumber to come back here immediately, Bobby,' she said. 'Hurry up now.'

Bobby had no difficulty in finding Flower Cottage because Impy lead him straight there. He knocked at the front door and, sure enough, the little man opened it, still wearing the same colourful clothes and the bobble-hat.

'Good morning,' said Bobby, breath-lessly. 'I've brought Impy home, and PLEASE will you come at once and put our bathroom back to normal.'

'Ah, so you realise now how nice it is to wash and bath regularly in lovely fresh water do you?' asked the little man, with a mischievous smile.

'Certainly I do,' said Bobby. 'But PLEASE don't waste time talking. My mother is desperate.'

The little man fetched his striped wand, waved it in the air, and announced:

> *'Swoon-sweam,*
> *Pour pure your stream.'*

Then he added, 'There is no need for me to accompany you home. From this moment your bathroom is as it was, except that the basin tap no longer drips. And will you please take this letter to your mother.'

'Certainly I will,' said Bobby. 'And thank you very much.'

He rushed back home, clutching the envelope, to find his mother standing at the front door.

'Our bathroom is all right again,' she

cried. 'I just turned on all the taps and they ran water.'

'I thought they would,' said Bobby. 'The plumber waved his magic wand and told them to.'

Then he handed his mother the envelope, which was addressed to her personally. It was typed on printed notepaper, and this is what it said:

From: Mr Handiman Hackentapp
Flower Cottage
Leafy Lane
(But don't call there because it has a habit of disappearing!)

JOBS OF ALL KINDS UNDERTAKEN BY MAGIC

Dear Madam,

This letter is to inform you that my magic will be available to the Brewster family, free, for the rest of the current year. By January 1st next year you will have experienced enough magic and I shall then pass it on to another family.

Should you require my services in any capacity, all you have to do is to telephone the firm you would normally employ for any particular job, using their number with the magic prefix 54321. You will then find that I am working at *that* time for *that* firm and I will come immediately, always with my dog Impy, to deal with your request.

On no account must this arrangement be disclosed to anyone outside the Brewster family. If it is, my magic will be withdrawn for ever.

I am, dear Madam,
Your obedient servant,
(Signed) Handiman Hackentapp

'What an extraordinary letter,' said Mrs Brewster. 'And what a fascinating name – Handiman Hackentapp. And there's no doubt about it, he really is magic. If Father agrees, I think we should take up his offer sometimes, don't you?'

'I certainly do,' agreed Bobby. 'Especially as in his letter he says that he will always bring Impy with him.'

CHAPTER TWO

The washing machine

When Bobby's father came home he was naturally surprised to read the letter. He had never met Handiman Hackentapp or Impy, so he was rather doubtful about the magic. He said that, whilst Bobby and his mother could use the services of Handiman Hackentapp if they wished, he would prefer to wait and see. As it turned out he soon had to sample some Handiman Hackentapp magic, himself without asking for it.

Bobby's mother was very proud of her new washing machine, but one morning it started making groaning noises.

'Oh dear,' she said to Bobby. 'I shall have to send for a man at once.'

Then they had the same idea together

and said in one voice, 'Handiman Hacken-tapp.'

Bobby begged his mother to allow him to dial the number because he was anxious to find if the magic code would work. The number of the suppliers of the machine was 31479, so he carefully dialled 54321/31479 and was pleased to hear the ringing tone. A lady's voice answered, and when Bobby explained the trouble she said, 'Oh dear, that won't do, will it? And luckily the mechanic for that particular brand is with us at the moment. I will send him round straight away.'

'I wonder?' said Bobby to his mother.

They didn't have to wonder long because in a few minutes they heard the tinkling bell, and there was Handiman Hackentapp on his purple tricycle, with Impy trotting beside him. So the magic code *had* worked!

He doffed his bobble-hat with a deep bow and Impy woofed three times. 'Good morning, madam,' he said, 'I understand that you have trouble with your washing machine.'

'I have indeed,' replied Mrs Brewster, and led him into the kitchen, where she switched on the machine. Immediately it groaned.

'It sounds as if it has a pain in its tummy doesn't it?' suggested Bobby.

Mr Hackentapp put on a listening face, and Impy cocked his head on one side and woofed three times: 'Woof – woof – woof.'

'It undoubtedly *has* got a pain,' agreed Mr Hackentapp. Then he took his striped wand from its zip bag, tapped the machine firmly three times, and announced:

> *'Twix-twerks,*
> *Come clear your works.'*

There was a rattling noise and something fell to the floor.

'And so would *you* have a pain in your tummy if *this* was in your works,' he

added, picking up a large safety pin! Then he turned to Mrs Brewster. 'Do you enjoy using this machine, madam?' he asked.

'I prefer it to my old machine,' she replied.

'I am delighted to hear it,' said Mr Hackentapp. 'And what about the clothes themselves? Are you satisfied with the condition in which they come from the machine?'

'Everything looks very clean, if that's what you mean,' said Mrs Brewster, 'though sometimes I wish we had the courage to wear more exciting clothes like yours, in dazzling colours. Especially my husband. He *never* wears anything colourful. Even his pyjamas are in old-fashioned stripes.'

Handiman Hackentapp exchanged glances with Impy, tapped the washing machine three more times with his wand, accompanied as usual with three Impy woofs, and announced:

'Pish-posh,
Bring bright your wash.'

'There, madam,' he said. 'If you will kindly test this machine whilst I am here I am sure that afterwards, when you fill it with clothes, everything will be to your complete satisfaction.'

Mrs Brewster switched on, and the machine made a noise that sounded as if it was delighted to be running smoothly again.

'Thank you very much,' she said. 'Before you leave, would you like a cup of coffee?'

'That's very kind of you, madam,' was the reply. 'It would be most refreshing.'

'Black or white?' asked Mrs Brewster.

'Purple, please,' said Mr Hackentapp.

'I beg your pardon?' asked Mrs Brewster.

'Purple please, madam,' repeated Mr Hackentapp.

'I'm afraid we have no purple coffee,' said Mrs Brewster.

'I think, when you pour on the boiling water, you will find that you have, madam,' Mr Hackentapp assured her.

And she had! Although her own cup filled with the usual brown coffee, Mr Hackentapp's *was* bright purple!

'Sugar?' she asked.

'I prefer salt,' replied Mr Hackentapp.

By then she was beyond surprise, so she asked as a matter of course, 'How many spoonfuls?'

'Six, please,' said Mr Hackentapp.

'I've never seen anyone drink purple coffee with six spoonfuls of salt in it,' said Mrs Brewster chattily, as she added spoonful after spoonful.

'No madam, I don't suppose you have,' said Handiman Hackentapp. 'But then you have never seen anyone like me before, have you?'

'That's perfectly true,' agreed Mrs Brewster.

Whilst the grown-ups were sipping their coffee – and Mr Hackentapp did so with evident relish – Bobby and Impy played together out in the garden. Bobby had never enjoyed a game of hide and seek so much before, though Impy seemed able to disappear at will, which made it difficult for the seeker. Bobby didn't mind. Impy nuzzled with his cold nose in such an enchanting way when he *did* manage to catch him. So a good time was had by all, both indoors and out, until Mr Hackentapp paid his usual respects to Mrs Brewster by bowing deeply and doffing his bobble-hat to the ground.

'Thank you for the coffee, madam,' he said, and then tinkled off on his tricycle with Impy trotting beside him.

'Do you know,' said Mrs Brewster eagerly, when they had gone, 'for once I'm really looking forward to doing the washing.'

Little did she realise. She filled the machine with a load of washing and switched on. It started with a gentle whirr, and the clothes turned over smoothly. Then the whirr changed to music, and very tuneful music it was too. Bobby heard it, and when he ran into the kitchen they joined hands and danced round together with the rhythm.

'Now you have a musical washing machine,' cried Bobby.

'I certainly have,' said his mother. 'And it will cheer up all my washing days in future, thanks to Handiman Hackentapp.'

But their surprise was by no means

over. When the music and machine stopped Mrs Brewster tipped out the clean washing and all the clothes were in dazzling colours, exactly as she had told Mr Hackentapp she would sometimes like to wear. Her dresses were assorted in gorgeous shades, and Bobby had T-shirts of all colours. Even the underclothes were coloured, and Bobby took an instant liking to his pink pants.

But by far the most impressive of all were Mr Brewster's pyjamas, which were bright crimson with two golden dragons – one on the front and the other on the back. Mrs Brewster held them up to their full length.

'These are the most staggering pyjamas I have ever seen,' she said. 'But I wonder whether your father will approve of them?'

'I doubt it,' said Bobby. 'And what about his shirts? They are brighter than those he usually wears, aren't they?'

'They certainly are,' agreed his mother.

'I think perhaps that it would be wise to break it to him gently.'

That is what she did. On the following evening, when they were sitting relaxed and satisfied together after a good meal, she said to her husband as casually as she could, 'By the way, dear, my washing machine went wrong yesterday, and can you guess who came to mend it? Handiman Hackentapp – and he made it more effective than it has ever been before.'

She thought that she would leave it at that for the time being. Then, just before they retired to bed, she took his crimson and gold pyjamas from the airing cupboard and laid them quietly out on his pillow.

'What on earth are these?' he cried, when he unfolded them to display their full glory, 'Have you bought me some new pyjamas?'

'No dear,' she replied soothingly, 'They are your old pyjamas exactly as they came out of the washing machine after Mr

Hackentapp had mended it, I told him I liked colourful clothes.'

'They will make me look ridiculous,' protested her husband.

'They will suit you splendidly,' she assured him. 'Why not try them on and see.'

Mr Brewster donned his pyjamas and looked at himself in the glass. 'How do I look?' he asked, preening himself.

'Very fetching, dear,' was the reply. 'They take years off your age.'

And as he admired himself he began to agree with her.

'At least they add a little colour to life,' he admitted, and his wife hoped that he would feel the same way in the morning when he saw his shirts.

At first he didn't. It's one thing to go to bed wearing brilliant pyjamas and another altogether going to the office dressed in dazzling shirts. But when he tried one on and looked in the mirror he began to flatter himself that the pink and grey stripes *did* make him look younger, so he decided to risk it.

It was a huge success. All his colleagues complimented him on his smartness, and the girls in the office asked each other, 'What *has* happened to Mr Brewster? He's suddenly "with it"!'

And that was true of the whole Brewster family. Somehow the extra colours in their clothes cheered them all up enormously.

So Handiman Hackentapp had really lived up to his promise to bring magic to the Brewster family, hadn't he? And that night Bobby's father announced at the supper table that he would certainly call for Handiman Hackentapp's services as soon as something needed doing.

CHAPTER THREE

Garden tools

Mr Brewster was true to his word, and the chance came when he remembered one afternoon that it was time for his garden tools to be looked at before the growing season started.

He telephoned the Garden Services, using the magic prefix number, and a man's voice said, 'We're very busy at this time of the year, sir, but we will certainly send *someone* round as soon as possible, though I am not sure who at the moment.'

Would it be? Could it be? Yes, indeed it could. The magic started immediately because the tinkling tricycle bell could be heard as soon as Mr Brewster put down the receiver.

'Well, at least he's prompt, whether his

magic is any good or not,' said Mr Brewster.

Then he caught sight of Handiman Hackentapp and Impy entering the drive. 'Goodness gracious me,' he said. 'He certainly *looks* magic enough. And what a perky little dog!'

Mr Hackentapp jumped off his tricycle.

'Good afternoon, sir,' he said, bowing deeply and trailing his bobble-hat to the floor. 'I presume that I have the pleasure of addressing Mr Brewster.'

'You have,' replied Mr Brewster, his eyes boggling.

'I am delighted to make your acquaintance, sir,' continued Mr Hackentapp. 'I have already assisted your wife and son on two occasions and trust that my efforts met with their complete approval.'

'They certainly did,' Mr Brewster assured him. 'That is why I dialled your special number.'

'I am most flattered to hear it,' said Handiman Hackentapp. 'And now in what respect can I be of service to you?'

'You can come into my shed and look at my garden tools,' replied Mr Brewster. 'Then, if you think that anything needs repairing or sharpening, please make arrangements to do it.'

'Once I have completed my inspection, sir,' Mr Hackentapp said, 'I am sure that no repairs or sharpening will be necessary.'

'Will you need Impy to help you this time, Mr Hackentapp?' asked Bobby eagerly. 'If not I would love to play with him in the garden while you are performing your magic in the shed. That is, if you don't mind.'

'Not in the least,' agreed Mr Hackentapp. 'And perhaps, whilst you are playing with Impy, he will perform some magic of his own.'

'Oh, *thank* you,' cried Bobby, and he and Impy ran happily away together.

At the bottom of the garden is a patch of ground which is supposed to be Bobby's own, but I'm afraid that he does not take much trouble, and it has turned into a wilderness of weeds.

Then, last Christmas, Aunt Angela presented the Brewster family with a plastic gnome sitting on a plastic toadstool to ornament their garden. Actually they do not like plastic gnomes, on or off toadstools, but they thought they had better put him outside somewhere in case Aunt Angela came unexpectedly to see them. Bobby offered to put the unwanted gnome on his own patch, and there he has been, sitting on his toadstool ever since, surrounded by weeds and looking sorry for himself.

And it was there that Impy found him whilst he and Bobby were romping in the garden that afternoon. Impy cocked his head on one side, woofed three times at the gnome; 'Woof-woof-woof,' and then darted straight back to Handiman Hackentapp in the shed, leaving Bobby to follow him, looking mystified.

In the meantime, to Mr Brewster's

amazement, Handiman Hackentapp had been busy in the shed tapping everything with his striped wand and saying his magic words. He had started with the mechanical tools.

To the electric hedge-cutter – of which Mr Brewster is very proud but he can't use it properly – he said:

> *'Snidge-snedge,*
> *your hedge,'*

and to the motor mower:

> *'Prune-prawn,*
> *Sheer smooth your lawn.'*

Mr Brewster stood there with a glazed expression on his face, looking as if he couldn't believe what he was seeing.

Just as Impy trotted into the shed, closely followed by Bobby, Handiman Hackentapp turned his attention to the other garden tools, and Impy seemed interested in them as well. He cocked his head on one side, and woofed three times as his master tapped the spade and fork three times each with his magic wand and said:

'*Tag-tig,*
Down deep your dig.'

'There, sir,' he said as he finished. 'I am sure that you will find that all your tools will work in the garden to your complete satisfaction.'

'But you haven't tested them yet!' protested Mr Brewster.

'Nevertheless, sir,' persisted Handiman Hackentapp, 'what I have done will prove quite sufficient to ensure their efficiency, and I now leave them in your capable hands.'

Mr Brewster made no reply. At that moment his wife came breezing into the shed and enquired, 'How are you getting on, dear?'

Mr Brewster was still speechless but Mr Hackentapp replied, 'Splendidly, Madam. Our labours are now complete.'

'Then in that case perhaps I can offer you a cup of coffee before you leave,' suggested Mrs Brewster.

'You can indeed, madam,' said Handiman Hackentapp. 'Your last brew was delicious.'

They went into the house and Mrs Brewster asked hesitatingly, 'Black, white, or purple?'

'Pink, please,' replied Mr Hackentapp.

'Did you say *pink*?' asked Mr Brewster.

'Yes sir, pink,' repeated Mr Hackentapp as Mrs Brewster poured hot water into a cup containing a spoonful of her usual coffee essence, which immediately turned pink.

'Sugar – or salt?' she asked.

'Soda please, madam,' said Mr Hackentapp.

'Did you say *soda*?' asked Mr Brewster.

'Yes sir, soda,' repeated Mr Hackentapp, and added, 'eight spoonfuls please.'

'Did you say *eight*?' asked Mr Brewster.

'Yes sir, eight,' repeated Mr Hackentapp. 'I always like pink coffee well soda'd.'

'Well I never,' gasped Mr Brewster, and lapsed into silence – from which he never recovered until Mr Hackentapp drank his pink coffee and took his leave.

'Goodbye, madam. Goodbye, sir,' he said, bowing deeply as usual and doffing his bobble-hat. Then he jumped on to his purple tricycle and rode away with Impy trotting beside him.

'There you are,' said Mrs Brewster. 'Didn't we tell you that he was magic?'

'Yes, but not magic like that,' replied her husband. 'Pink coffee and eight spoonfuls of soda indeed! And I shan't know if his magic is any good until I use my garden tools tomorrow.'

But even before that, during the night, something peculiar happened. Bobby thought that he could distinctly hear the sound of digging in the garden, and at breakfast he mentioned it to his parents.

'*I* heard that too,' said his mother. 'I thought I was dreaming.'

'*I* heard it as well,' said his father. 'Let's go outside and look.'

The first thing they noticed was the plastic gnome sitting on his toadstool, whereas before he had been hidden by

41

weeds. Then they found that the whole of Bobby's plot had been neatly dug up and the weeds were thrown on top of the compost heap.

'Look at that gnome,' cried Bobby. 'His shoes are covered with mud, and so are the spade and fork leaning against his toad-stool.'

'Then *he* must have done the digging,' said Mrs Brewster. 'It's more Hackentapp magic.'

'And Impy's,' said Bobby. 'And useful magic too. It has saved me the trouble of tidying my garden.'

'Perhaps we had better use the other tools,' suggested Mr Brewster to his wife. 'I will try the hedge-cutter and you mow the lawn.'

He fetched the garden steps so that he could reach the top of the hedge and went to plug in the hedge-cutter lead. Then, when he switched on, amazing things started happening. He found himself trimming the top of the hedge at a furious pace,

in a perfect straight line, whilst the steps staggered beneath his feet.

'Help!' he cried. Then he fell off the steps and let go of the hedge-cutter. But it didn't fall. It continued trimming the hedge all on its own. Even when he switched it off it made no difference.

But even more amazing things were happening on the back lawn. Bobby's mother had pulled the toggle to start the mower and it roared away, pulling her behind it, completely out of control. All she could do was to run behind it shouting 'HELP!' Then she let go of the handle and off it ran without her. She followed it, but when it reached the edge of the lawn it turned round and chased her back to the other side. She ran in panic like a rabbit until she had the sense to swerve out of its way. Then it turned round at the other edge and roared back again until it became clear that, without anyone steering it, it was mowing the lawn on its own!

But what was going to happen when the hedge-cutter reached the end of the hedge and the lawn-mover the far end of the lawn? Bobby was frantic when he saw his father fall off the steps and his mother being chased by the lawn-mower. What could he do?

Then he had an idea. He ran inside and dialled the Garden Service with the magic prefix. At first there was no reply but then the ringing tone stopped and he asked, 'Who is there please?'

'Woof-woof-woof,' came a bark from the other end.

'I beg your pardon?' asked Bobby Brewster.

'Woof-woof-woof,' repeated the bark, and then Bobby realised who it was.

'Please come here at once, Impy,' he cried. 'Mr Hackentapp's magic is out of control.'

There was silence and Bobby ran outside, where his mother and father were gazing at the garden tools which were still furiously cutting the hedge and mowing the lawn. Could they ever be stopped?

Yes, they could. Just as the top of the hedge was completely trimmed and the mower reached the far corner of the back lawn, along the drive ran Impy. He took a quick look at the hedge-cutter, cocked his head on one side and woofed: 'Woof-woof-woof,' and, lo and behold, the hedge-cutter stopped cutting and dropped gently to the ground without coming to any harm.

Then Impy ran to the back lawn, cocked his head on one side, and woofed three times at the lawn-mower, which came to rest at the top corner of the lawn. The Brewster family sighed with relief, Impy barked a parting woof, and, before Bobby could catch him he trotted away and disappeared down the road.

'Phew!' gasped Mr Brewster. 'Just in time. What a lucky thing that Impy arrived at that moment.'

'It wasn't luck,' said Bobby. 'I spoke to him on the telephone and asked him to come.'

'You did *what*?' cried his father.

'I dialled the Hackentapp Special Garden Service number and Impy answered at the other end with three woofs,' explained Bobby. 'So I asked him to come round immediately.'

'Well, now I've heard everything,' exclaimed Mr Brewster. 'And I certainly agree with you that Handiman Hackentapp and Impy are both truly magic.'

CHAPTER FOUR

Bedroom wallpaper

'It's about time that your bedroom wall-paper was replaced, Bobby,' said his mother one morning. 'I wonder if your father could be persuaded to do it?'

'Oh *please* not,' cried Bobby. 'You know how long he takes. He gets all the joins wrong and covers himself with paste and it puts him in a bad temper. Why not ask Handiman Hackentapp?'

'Of course,' agreed his mother. 'Fancy forgetting Mr Hackentapp! I'll ring him up at once.'

The decorator's number was 32666 so she rang 54321/32666.

Mrs Brewster did not recognise the answering man's voice. 'Hullo, can I help you?' he asked.

'Yes I think so,' she replied. 'Can you send someone round to make arrangements about papering a bedroom?'

'Certainly, madam,' replied the voice – and immediately rang off.

'You don't know who I am yet!' cried Mrs Brewster, but by then the line was dead.

'Silly man,' said Mrs Brewster.

But he wasn't silly at all. They did not have to wait long. Mr Hackentapp and Impy arrived in next to no time.

'Good morning, Madam,' he said, with the usual bow and sweep of his bobble-hat. 'I understand that my services are required today in a paperhanging capacity. Where, may I ask, am I to employ my skill?'

'In Bobby's bedroom,' replied Mrs Brewster.

'What better place for magic than the sleeping quarters of my young friend,' said Mr Hackentapp, and they all trooped upstairs.

'Ah, yes,' said Mr Hackentapp, 'I feel

sure that we can improve upon this. What type of pattern do you favour? A picturesque countryside design, perhaps?'

'Or seaside,' suggested Mrs Brewster.

'Or railway trains,' added Bobby.

'Why not combine all three?' suggested Mr Hackentapp. 'It is popular these days. Cover three walls with different scenes and leave the other wall plain.'

'That's a good idea,' said Mrs Brewster.

'Then it is agreed I presume, madam,' continued Handiman Hackentapp. 'And now, may I ask, do you possess any sheets of brown paper?'

'There are some in the cupboard under the stairs,' answered Mrs Brewster, wondering why they were required.

'Then perhaps you will be kind enough to bring them here,' said Handiman Hackentapp. 'I see no reason why we should not proceed at once.'

'But you have no table or sticky paste,' protested Bobby.

'I have my magic wand, and that is all I

require,' Mr Hackentapp assured him, and he proceeded to unzip his bag whilst Mrs Brewster ran to fetch the brown paper.

'I'm afraid there's not nearly enough of this to cover the walls,' she said when she returned.

'That is of no consequence whatever, madam,' replied Handiman Hackentapp. 'Please unfold the top sheet and lay it on the floor.'

She did as she was asked. Mr Hackentapp tapped it three times with his wand and announced:

> *'Flittern-flattern,*
> *Paint pretty your pattern.'*

Immediately the sheet of paper was covered with the most attractive country scene.

'Now I have to be more careful with the next step,' said Mr Hackentapp. 'And I need your assistance, madam. Will you please face the wall and hold the paper as

flat as you can with the picture facing you.
Then, when I say my magic words, throw
it towards the wall with your hands apart.'

'Certainly,' said Mrs Brewster, though
she looked far from certain as she said it.
Mr Hackentapp tapped the wall three
times with his wand and said:

> *'Twee-twow,*
> *Straight sure her throw.'*

and she flung away the paper. As if by magnetism it flew towards the wall, expanding as it did so, and there was the wall completely covered with the lovely countryside scene.

'Now for the next wall,' announced Handimann Hackentapp confidently, and the whole process was repeated, except that when he made his taps and said his magic words a different pattern appeared on the paper. This time it was a railway scene with a jolly old engine, pulling old-fashioned carriages, puffing along a track. Bobby had never been in a train like that before and his first thought, as he gazed in wonderment at his bedroom wall, was that he would be able to lie in bed imagining that he was a passenger.

And there was more to come. In exactly the same way, helped by his mother's unerring aim, the third wall was covered with a seaside scene, with cliffs and rocks and blue water and children running along the sands doing exactly what Bobby liked doing when he was on holiday.

But this time Impy did not seem satisfied. He cocked his head on one side, and woofed: 'Woof-woof-woof.' Hey presto! there on the sands was a little dog looking exactly like Impy. It almost seemed as if he had woofed himself on to the wall – except that he was still there in the bedroom!

Covering the last wall seemed simple because it only needed plain paper. But curiously enough his mother made her first mistake. When she threw the sheet of brown paper it stuck to the window instead of the wall and had to be peeled away. She apologised profusely, and although Handimann Hackentapp accepted her apology, Bobby had the impression that he had arranged the false throw on purpose just to show that the whole thing was his magic and not hers!

Anyway, her second throw was more successful, and Bobby thought that the plain wall made the three patterns look more beautiful than ever.

There was silence as Bobby and his mother took in the general effect. Then Mrs Brewster could contain herself no longer.

'That is wonderful, Mr Hackentapp,' she cried. 'And you deserve the best cup of coffee I have ever made. What is it to be this time? Black – white – purple – or pink?'

'Green with yellow stripes, please, madam,' was the reply. And, believe it or not, that is what she made. She purposely put the coffee essence into a tumbler and, when the water was added, there was the coffee clearly showing its vivid green and

yellow stripes through the glass. She was so surprised that she forgot to ask what to add, so Mr Hackentapp had to ask for himself.

'Please sprinkle it profusely with pepper, madam,' he said, and, still speechless, she did as he requested. Then he drank his striped peppered coffee with relish, paid his usual bowing respects, and rode away on his tricycle with Impy trotting beside him.

They could hardly wait for Mr Brewster to return home from work that evening, and as soon as he opened the front door he was proudly ushered upstairs to view Bobby's bedroom.

'Good heavens,' he said. 'Who is responsible for this?' Then he added quickly 'Don't tell me – it's Handiman Hackentapp again!'

'What do you think of it?' asked his wife.

'Magnificent,' he said. 'But how did he manage to do it so quickly?'

'He didn't do it all himself,' replied Mrs

Brewster proudly, 'I helped him. He waved his magic wand and said his magic words and asked me to throw the paper at the wall – and there it stuck.'

'Did he indeed?' mused Mr Brewster. 'Perhaps he might give *me* a few lessons some time.'

'It wouldn't do any good – you would still cover yourself with paste, dear,' said his wife.

One last funny thing happened later. When Bobby was in bed studying the seaside wall, there was Impy the dog rushing about on the sands and darting in and out of the sea. And when he came out of the water he really did look wet! So he really must have woofed himself on to the wallpaper.

And he was having such a lovely time at the seaside that Bobby fell asleep dreaming of his own summer holidays which were soon to come.

CHAPTER FIVE

The music room

One of the rooms in the Brewster house is called the music room. It was given the rather grand title because it contained an old upright piano, seldom used and badly out of tune, and also a violin and a flute; instruments which Mr and Mrs Brewster learned at school and had never touched since.

At school Bobby learns the recorder and he enjoys it. One afternoon at home, his mother listened to his playing and said, 'My word, Bobby, you *have* got on.'

'I love music at school,' said Bobby. Then his mother had an idea.

'How would you like to have piano lessons?' she asked.

'I would love it,' cried Bobby. Later his

father agreed, but he said, 'We must first have our piano tuned. Do you know of anyone locally who could do it?'

With one voice Bobby and his mother suggested Handiman Hackentapp.

On the following morning Mrs Brewster rang the number of the local music shop, with the prefix 54321, and was surprised to hear the voice of Mr Hackentapp himself, although he had never been seen in the music shop before.

When she explained what she wanted he said, 'Certainly madam, I will be at your service in a piano tuning capacity this very afternoon.'

True to his promise he was, accompanied, of course, by Impy. When he examined the old piano he said, 'This instrument looks rather neglected, madam.'

'I'm afraid it is,' agreed Mrs Brewster. 'It hasn't been used for years.'

Then Handiman Hackentapp asked Impy to jump on the keyboard and run up and down all the keys, and it sounded awful! Most of the notes were badly out of tune and some didn't sound at all.

'Oh dear,' said Mrs Brewster, and Bobby felt anxious in case the piano was beyond repair.

'No matter, madam, I can cope with it,' said Handiman Hackentapp. He took his magic wand from the zip-bag, touched the keys, both black and white (all 85 of them) and announced:

> *'Tweets-twotes,*
> *Play pure your notes,'*

accompanied by three Impy woofs.

Then he sat down and played a sprightly dance so expertly that Bobby and his mother joined hands and danced round the room together. When he stopped Mrs Brewster said breathlessly, 'My word – you *are* a lovely pianist, Mr Hackentapp.'

'It is one of my many accomplishments, madam,' he agreed.

'I hope that Bobby will be able to play as

well as that one day,' she said.

'I'm sure he will, madam,' said Mr Hackentapp. 'Given suitable tuition.'

'Can you recommend anybody?' asked Mrs Brewster.

'Indeed I can, madam,' was the reply.

'Who?' asked Mrs Brewster.

'Myself,' said Mr Hackentapp.

'So you can *teach* the piano as well as play it,' said Mrs Brewster.

'Only to specially selected pupils, madam,' said Mr Hackentapp, 'amongst whom this young gentleman can certainly be included. And then on one strict condition. I refuse to allow my pupils to achieve excellence too easily. He must apply himself and promise to practise at least half an hour each day.'

'Of course,' cried Bobby, 'I promise.'

'Very well,' agreed Handiman Hackentapp, 'I will come at 6.00 pm every Tuesday and Friday to give lessons.'

Before he left Mrs Brewster, as usual, offered Mr Hackentapp some coffee. To her surprise, when asked what colour, he replied, 'Normal brown coffee please, madam.'

'Milk or cream?' she asked.

'Cream please, madam,' was the reply, and she thought that for once he would be drinking ordinary and not magic coffee. But not for long, because he added 'Salad cream if you please, madam, and plenty of it!'

And when he had drunk the extraordinary concoction he thanked his hostess by doffing his bobble-hat, and he and Impy departed the usual way.

Needless to say, Handiman Hackentapp proved to be an excellent piano teacher, and within a few weeks Bobby was beginning to play real tunes with both hands, and his parents were proud of him. So was Impy, who woof-woof-woofed with appreciation each time he played correctly. Then one afternoon, when all the Brewsters were at home, Mr Hackentapp noticed the flute and violin on the shelf in the music room.

'I see that you are the possessors of other musical instruments,' he said.

'Yes,' replied Mrs Brewster. 'The violin is mine.'

'And the flute is mine,' added Mr Brewster.

'We both learned them at school and have never played since,' they explained.

'Oh dear,' said Handiman Hackentapp.

'Then I had better put them in good working order.'

He touched the violin with his wand and
said:

> 'Flangs-flings,
> Sound sweet your strings.'

Then he touched the flute with his wand
and said:

> 'Tweets-twoots,
> Toot tuneful toots.'

accompanied, of course, by three Impy
woofs each time.

Then Mr Hackentapp picked them up
one after another and played a beautiful
melody on each.

'Goodness gracious,' they cried. 'What
an expert musician you are!'

'I am generally considered to be,' agreed
Mr Hackentapp. 'And may I suggest that,
after giving your son piano lessons twice

each week, I also give you tuition on your own instruments. Then you can form a family trio and charm the people of the neighbourhood.'

'That's a splendid idea,' said Mr Brewster. 'But I'm afraid that neither of us can spare enough time for half an hour's practise each day, and I am sometimes away altogether.'

'No matter, sir,' said Handiman Hackentapp. 'I appreciate your difficulty and will apply more concentrated magic with your lessons to allow you to learn more quickly than your son.'

From then on the music lessons continued for all the Brewsters, twice a week, and not only did Bobby come to enjoy his regular practice, but his mother and father found time, though not for so long. Within a few weeks Bobby really *did* play pure notes on his piano, his mother really *did* sound sweet strings on her violin, and his father really *did* toot tuneful toots on the flute.

After a time they were playing trios by well-known composers like Mozart and Beethoven – and sometimes even a pop tune – conducted by Handiman Hackentapp and applauded by Impy woofs. Indeed, their neighbours heard them playing and they became well known in the district.

So much so that, later in the year, large posters were on display all over the place advertising a concert in aid of Bobby's school music funds, and this is what they announced:

SPECIAL ATTRACTION
RECITAL BY THE
FAMOUS
BREWSTER TRIO

And at the end of that concert the applause was deafening, not only from a packed audience, but also from loud WOOFS by Impy at the back of the hall.

So that is how Handiman Hackentapp and Impy used their magic to introduce the Brewster family to the true magic of music, and also how the music room in the Brewster house came to live up to its name.

CHAPTER SIX

Dirty windows

'I do wish that our window-cleaner would come,' said Mrs Brewster one evening. 'He's supposed to be here once a month and it's far longer than that since his last visit.'

'Why not ring him up and remind him?' suggested her husband.

So she did, and found to her dismay that the window-cleaner had fallen off his ladder and broken a leg. He would not be back at work for some time.

'Oh dear,' she said. 'Poor man – I'm sorry I criticised him. But what are we to do? Window-cleaners are hard to find, and I don't trust you up a ladder, dear. Our windows are in such a state that we can hardly see the remaining flowers out in the

67

garden before they fade.'

'Why not try Handiman Hackentapp?' suggested Mr Brewster.

'Do you think he would mind?' asked Mrs Brewster. 'He usually does skilled work like tuning pianos and mending washing machines and garden tools. I would hate him to feel insulted by being asked just to clean windows.'

'We can but try,' urged Mr Brewster. 'He *did* say in his letter "Jobs of all kinds undertaken by magic". Let me ring him.'

'Very well,' agreed Mrs Brewster, 'but do be tactful.'

So Mr Brewster rang the window cleaner's number again, but this time with the prefix 54321.

'Hullo,' answered a lady's voice.

'Is that the window-cleaner's house?' asked Mr Brewster.

'Yes,' was the reply, 'and I will arrange for my husband to come tomorrow morning.'

And the lady rang off without enquiring

who had made the request.

'Well, there was certainly something magic about that call,' said Mr Brewster.

On the following morning the tinkling bell was heard and Handiman Hackentapp made his usual colourful appearance with Impy.

'Good morning, madam, sir, and Master Robert,' he said to the assembled Brewsters, making his usual bow. 'I report here in a window-cleaning capacity.'

'I hope you don't mind,' said Mrs Brewster anxiously.

'Why should I, madam?' replied Mr Handiman Hackentapp. 'As I told you in my letter my services are available in any capacity to the Brewster family until the end of the year, when they will be withdrawn and offered elsewhere.'

'Thank you for coming so soon. I hope your wife doesn't object to your working on a Saturday,' said Mr Brewster.

'I'm not a married man, sir,' said Mr Hackentapp.

'But the lady on the telephone told me yesterday that she would hand on my message to her window-cleaning husband,' said Mr Brewster.

'That was me, pretending to be my wife,' explained Mr Hackentapp.

'Why?' asked Mr Brewster.

'Because then if I receive a request for my husband to perform a task which he doesn't wish to perform I forget, as Mrs Hackentapp, to pass on the message to myself as Mr Hackentapp, so Mr Hackentapp knows nothing about it. It is very convenient.'

'I'm sure it is,' agreed Mrs Brewster. 'Anyway, I'm glad that Mrs Hackentapp passed on the message to her husband this time because our windows are in a frightful state. We can hardly see our garden flowers through the sitting-room window, and they will soon fade away.'

'I can soon remedy that, madam,' Mr Hackentapp assured her.

'Be sure to be careful up the ladder,'

urged Mrs Brewster. 'Our poor regular window-cleaner fell off his and broke a leg.'

'I shall not require a ladder, madam,' said Mr Hackentapp.

'Then how will you clean the upstairs windows?' she asked.

'I shall fly up to them, madam,' replied Mr Hackentapp.

Which he promptly did, landing on the

window-sill outside Mr and Mrs Brewster's bedroom, carrying his magic striped wand. And, believe it or not, Impy did an enormous jump and landed right next to him.

Then Mr Hackentapp tapped all the upstairs windows in turn with his wand and said to each one:

'Flip-flew,
Plan picturesque view.'

followed every time by three Impy woofs.

After that they both jumped to the ground, landing gently, and repeated the process with the same words and woofs on all the downstairs windows. And, there was no doubt about it, when they had finished, all the windows in the house were just as clean and shining as if Handiman Hackentapp had spent many hours polishing them.

'Well,' said Mrs Brewster, 'after all that effort you deserve a cup of coffee. What colour would you like this time?'

'Madam,' was the reply, 'though it may not have been apparent to you, I have just completed a task so arduous that I am quite breathless with the exertion. Could you supply me with a cold drink, please?'

'Of course,' said Mrs Brewster. 'Lemonade, blackcurrant, or perhaps beer?'

'What I really would appreciate is a refreshing glass of vinegar,' said Mr Hackentapp. And when it was given to him he really did seem to find it refreshing!

Then off they went, he and Impy, in their usual tinkling and woofing way.

For the rest of the day it seemed to the Brewsters that, although Mr Hackentapp's window-cleaning had obviously been performed by magic, there was nothing more magical with the results than sparkling clean windows. But they had underestimated the magic handyman!

When Bobby came down to breakfast on the following morning he said, 'I had a marvellous time last night. When I was lying in bed I heard the engine on my wallpaper starting to puff, and when I looked up it had pulled the carriages right off the wall and on to my bedroom window. Then I jumped out of bed – at least, I *think* I did – and got into a carriage. Impy was there, and we had a wonderful train-ride together round and round the window all night through the most beautiful country. And in a first class carriage too!'

'You must have been dreaming,' said his mother.

'I'm not so sure,' said his father, 'because *I* heard a noise too, of a cricket bat hitting a ball, and when I looked at the window on my side of the bed there was a most exciting cricket match in progress.'

'*You* must have been dreaming too,' persisted his wife.

'I found that I was playing myself,' continued Mr Brewster. 'And when I went in to bat I made 106 not out!'

'Then you certainly *were* dreaming,' said his wife.

'Dreaming or not, it was a very exciting game,' said Mr Brewster. 'And all due, no doubt, to Handiman Hackentapp's magic window-cleaning.'

But that wasn't all. Mrs Brewster's own magic was to follow. When she opened the curtains of the sitting-room she cried, 'Just look at the lovely flowers in our garden! They are more beautiful than they have been throughout the summer.'

And they were, including flowers blooming that had never been planted, that they all saw through the window. But when they trooped out to the garden only the fading autumn flowers were there! So the window flowers were all due to Handiman Hackentapp's magic window-cleaning as well!

It was lasting magic, too, right through to the end of the year. As autumn turned into winter the window flowers bloomed more and more colourfully. Even on bitterly cold days the buds burst into flower and cheered the Brewsters up with the thought of sunny summer weather.

The special magic for Bobby and his father also continued throughout October, November and December. On at least two nights each week Bobby and Impy went for window train-rides together through different bits of beautiful country on each journey.

What is more, on every Saturday night Bobby's father played window cricket for his club against a different team each match. And, – even more remarkably – every time he went in to bat he made a century!

Which proved beyond doubt, Mr Brewster said, that Handiman Hackentapp was capable of performing the most magic magic ever!

CHAPTER SEVEN

New Year's Eve party

At the end of the Hackentapp year there was going to be rather an unusual holiday. The Brewster relations were coming over from Northern Ireland on December 29th to stay for a few days, so Mrs Brewster had an idea.

'I propose,' she said, 'that we spend Christmas quietly together, with just small presents on the day, and then have a grand combined Christmas and New Year's Eve party with all the usual Christmas food and trimmings.'

Then Mr Brewster had an even better idea. 'Why not ask Handiman Hackentapp to organise all the catering and evening entertainment?' he added. 'Then he can end his year with us with a flourish.'

'But will he perform his magic with other people there?' asked Mrs Brewster anxiously.

'I don't see why not,' replied her husband. 'After all, he did say that his magic was available to the Brewster family – and they are just as much Brewsters as we are.'

'We can but try,' she agreed.

So they dialled the number of the local caterers; with the magic prefix, of course.

At first the result looked unpromising. A voice at the other end said, 'Who do you want? You're ringing a public telephone box,' but then added: 'Oh, there's a funny little man knocking on the window, perhaps he's expecting you. I'll ask him.'

And of course it *was* Handiman Hackentapp, though how he could be expecting a call from the Brewsters at a public telephone box will never be known!

'Mr Hackentapp,' asked Mrs Brewster, 'could you organise a New Year's Eve party for us, with all the catering and evening entertainment? A very special party to celebrate the end of the year and your last day with us. And there will be others present; my husband's brother Derek, his wife Heather, and their daughter Barbara.'

'I shall be delighted to exercise my final magic for the benefit of any members of the Brewster family, madam,' Mr Hackentapp assured her.

'Good,' she said. 'Perhaps we should discuss the arrangements well in advance. Could you pop round to see me tomorrow?'

'It will be a pleasure to do so, madam,' was the reply.

And it was – to all concerned. But perhaps most of all to Bobby, who had his longest and best game in the garden with Impy whilst his mother and Handiman Hackentapp were having their cooking discussion in the kitchen.

'As far as the turkey and Christmas pudding are concerned, you can leave all the preparation to me,' said Handiman

Hackentapp. 'I will arrive at one o'clock with your complete meal ready cooked.'

'Excellent,' said Mrs Brewster.

'The Christmas cake and extras, like mince pies, will have to be cooked by you in advance,' continued Mr Hackentapp. 'I think I should exercise some of my magic in your kitchen before I leave. Will you please place all your cooking utensils on the table.'

Mrs Brewster did as she was asked whilst he took his magic wand from the zip-bag. Then he tapped everything, including the stove, with three distinct taps and said:

'Bleeps-blakes,
Bake beautiful cakes.'

This time he added some more words:

'For New Year's Eve.'

After that Handiman Hackentapp went

into all the rooms in the house waving his
magic wand and announcing clearly
everywhere:

> 'Pigic-pagic,
> Make everything magic,'

and every time he added, quite emphatically –
'On New Year's Eve.'

When all this was over Mrs Brewster
offered him some refreshment as usual.
'It's rather cold this morning,' she said, 'so
perhaps you would like some of your
coloured coffee?'

'This time, madam,' replied Mr Hackentapp, 'I should prefer tea.'

'Indian or China?' she asked.

'Dandelion please, madam,' he replied.

'I'm afraid that I have no dandelion tea in
the house,' she said.

'If you pour some boiling water on to
one of your teabags you will find that you
have, madam,' Handiman Hackentapp

assured her.

And she had. Complete with a few dandelion petals floating on the top to prove it. As he drank it he said, 'This is one of my favourite brews, madam. It is not only delicious to drink but also has medicinal qualities.' And he smacked his lips in appreciation.

Then he added, 'You need have no fears about your New Year's Eve festivities, madam. Not only will the food be delicious but our entire last day together will be memorably magic.'

He called Impy from the garden and off they went together with the usual bowing, tinkling and woofing.

The first signs that his remarks were true came when Mrs Brewster made the Christmas cake. She put all the ingredients in a bowl and then had to go and answer the front doorbell. When she returned to the kitchen everything in the bowl was ready mixed. She baked the cake in the oven and left it to cool, and on the follow-

ing morning there it was, neatly iced, with an attractive winter scene on top and the words:

A HAPPY NEW YEAR
TO ALL THE BREWSTERS

The mince pies came just as magically. They didn't even have to be put in the oven. After she had prepared them the telephone bell rang and when she came back they were already cooked!

The usual decorations were put up for

Christmas Day, but it was a quiet affair with only token presents because the real ones were saved for New Year's Eve. In bed that night Bobby had a special magic Christmas window train-ride with Impy through snow-covered scenery that looked like Switzerland – a real white Christmas. His father had an even more remarkable final window cricket match of the season during which he not only made another century but also took eight wickets!

The Northern Ireland Brewsters arrived as arranged, all looking well, especially cousin Barbara. New Year's Eve followed shortly, and when they first looked outside the garden was sparkling magic and snow covered. Bobby and Barbara played in the snow, and they built a lifelike snowman. In fact, Barbara thought that he must *be* alive because she distinctly saw him wink at her.

As one o'clock approached Mrs Brewster began to have qualms. Supposing

Handiman Hackentapp was ill and failed to turn up. What *would* they have for dinner? And how could he possibly bring all the food on his tricycle?

There was no need to worry of course. Bobby was pressing his nose against the window to watch for the approach of Handiman Hackentapp and Impy when the sound of a tinkling bell came from the sky and he looked upwards. A multi-coloured helicopter – or was it a fairycopter? – landed on the lawn. As the assembled company gazed in amazement the hood was opened and out jumped Impy, wagging his tail, followed by Handiman Hackentapp dressed as usual except that he wore a chef's tall white hat with a bobble on top! He was carrying a dish with a silver cover.

Bobby and his parents ran outside to help.

'Please ask your butler to announce to the assembled company that dinner is about to be served,' he said to Mrs Brewster.

'But we have no butler,' she protested.

'Oh yes you have, madam,' he replied, as he nodded to Impy who immediately woofed three times at the snowman: 'Woof-woof-woof.'

What do you think happened? The snowman drew himself up proudly and in a most impressive voice he announced, 'Ladies and Gentlemen. Dinner is served!'

And what a dinner it was! Delicious tender turkey expertly carved by the snowman butler, who showed no signs of

melting indoors, and all the usual veget-
ables and trimmings, served piping hot.
Barbara and Bobby broke the wishbone,
and Bobby won the wish. Can you guess
what it was? Ah – that would be telling!

Next came Christmas pudding, with
brandy set alight on top and silver coins
inside each helping, followed by those
mince pies that had cooked themselves and
tasted all the better for it.

After dinner presents were opened, and
everyone had *exactly* what they wanted.
But the funny thing was that the presents
were not what had been bought in the first
place. For instance, Bobby had bought a
doll for Barbara when she really hoped that
he would give her a book, and when she
opened her parcel it *was* the very book she
wanted most! And she had bought for
Bobby a set of draughts, which in fact he
already had, but when he opened her
present he found what he had longed for –
a conjuring set! This happened with other
people as well, but nobody ever let on. All

the recipients said, 'Thank you very much.
'It's *just* what I wanted,' which it was. And
all the givers kept quiet because they
hadn't bought what was wanted in the first
place! So everyone was completely satisfied, though mystified.

When dinner was over a hearty vote of
thanks was passed to Mr Handiman the
cook, Impy, and the snowman butler. The
grown-ups were told to go straight into
the sitting-room to sleep it off, for which
they passed an even heartier vote of thanks!

During the afternoon Barbara and Bobby romped with Impy in the snow. It was
great fun, but Bobby began to feel a sinking feeling in his tummy when he remembered that this was his last magic game
with Impy.

For tea they nibbled the delicious
Christmas cake, and for supper cold tur-
key, though no one was very hungry.
Then came the evening entertainment.

First to perform was the snowman butler, who juggled knives, forks, and spoons

expertly. Impy did fantastic gymnastics, and then came the magician. You can guess who that was, can't you? Handiman Hackentapp, of course. He produced all sorts of surprising things from even more surprising places. A silver ball was found in Bobby's ear, and Barbara was quite worried when she found that she had been sitting on a live rabbit! But the rabbit didn't seem to mind!

The Brewster trio then did their stuff, greatly admired by their Northern Ireland relations, and finally they sang choruses together, accompanied by Handiman Hackentapp on the piano, while Impy, nuzzling with his cold nose against Bobby's knees, howled with delight.

And it was then that Bobby's sinking feeling returned. The clock said half past eleven. In half-an-hour Handiman Hackentapp, the snowman butler, and Impy would be leaving for ever.

Bedtime drinks were proposed, and this gave Handiman Hackentapp the last

chance to display his magic powers. He brought from the kitchen a tray with glasses and cups and only one jug. Then he asked everyone what they would like best for their nightcap, and proceeded to pour out of that one jug whatever they asked for, hot or cold.

That was when Mrs Brewster summed

up everyone's feelings as she drank her hot chocolate.

'Do you know, Mr Hackentapp,' she said, 'today has been so packed with magic that I am full to the brim and could take no more.'

Handiman Hackentapp did not resent her remark. 'Madam,' he replied, 'That has been my deliberate intention. As you know, we leave at midnight. It has been a pleasure serving the Brewster family because their demands for my magic have never been excessive. From now on you will all have to produce your own magic, which, after all, is the most satisfying magic of all.'

And with that profound thought he took his leave, exactly as the clock was striking twelve. His morning helicopter *must* have been a fairycopter because it had disappeared, and his usual purple tricycle was by the garage.

'Goodbye, everybody,' he said, bowing deeply and doffing his chef's bobble-hat to the ground. 'And a Happy New Year to you all.'

The snowman butler followed him out into the garden and took up his place where he had been built that morning. Mr Hackentapp ran to his tricycle and mounted. But for the first time Impy followed his master reluctantly, licking Bobby affectionately on the hand before he went. For once there was no tinkling bell, woofing, or wagging of tail. They both left in silence, Impy with his tail between his legs.

But although the snow lay deep along the drive, not a wheel-mark or a paw-print was left behind as they turned into the road and disappeared.

Postscript

Bobby woke up on New Year's Day with that sinking feeling still in his tummy, and he looked sadly out of his bedroom window. The ground was still snow-covered, though there was only a mound of snow where the snowman butler had stood.

Along the drive, from road to garage, were the distinct paw-prints of a dog. Bobby dressed, ran downstairs, and opened the front door. Then he heard barking from the direction of the garage. He walked through the snow to open the garage door, and out jumped – who do you think? – Impy!

Bobby called to his mother, 'Look who I've found,' and she ran outside. Then he glanced at the name on Impy's collar and a look of sheer delight spread over his face.

'It's Impy's name, followed by my own name and address,' he cried. 'My wish-bone wish has come true. Impy is my very own dog.'

'So that is what you wished for,' said his

mother quietly, 'I wonder, now he belongs to you instead of Handiman Hackentapp, whether Impy is still magic?'

'No,' said Bobby emphatically, 'I'm sure he isn't. Last night when he left there were no pawmarks in the snow, but this morning on returning he has made the marks of an ordinary dog. And I am glad that he has. He may now be just an ordinary dog, but for him to be my very own is the most magical thing that has ever happened to both of us, isn't it Impy?'

Impy nuzzled to him with his cold nose, looked up trustingly at him, wagged his tail, and woofed three times in agreement: 'Woof – woof – woof.'

But this time they were just ordinary woofs.